FANGFACE:

A HEAP OF TROUBLE

CINNAMON HOUSE
A Division of Charter Communications, Inc.
A GROSSET & DUNLAP COMPANY

FANGFACE: A HEAP OF TROUBLE
Copyright © 1979 Ruby-Spears Productions, Inc.
A Filmways Company
All Rights Reserved
Fangface created and designed by Jerry Eisenberg for
Ruby-Spears Productions, Inc.
Illustrations by Tony Tallarico
Tempo Books is registered in the U.S. Patent Office
A Cinnamon House Edition
ISBN: 0-448-15890-6
Published simultaneously in Canada
Printed in the United States of America

FANGFACE: A HEAP OF TROUBLE

The Fangface gang runs into a heap of adventure when they set out to find the mysterious monster who is turning a college campus upside-down. Laugh along with Biff, Kim and Puggsy in the hilarious adventures of FANGFACE.

For extra fun, color the pictures as you read the book!

1

The quiet Midtown University campus was deserted at night. All but one of the buildings were totally dark. The one building that was lit was the Science Building. Four men were working in one of the laboratories.

The men stood in the lab. They were looking at a shiny new machine. Its buttons and knobs glowed as the machine made a soft whirring noise.

"At last, after years of hard work, our machine is completed," said the chief scientist. "You gentlemen are about to witness a breakthrough which will mean more to us than..."

His words were cut off by an ear-shattering roar. It was coming from the other side of the locked lab door.

2

"There's someone out there," said one of the scientists.

"Or something!" answered one of his friends.

Suddenly the lab door began to rattle. "Whatever it is, it's trying to get in!" cried the chief scientist.

"But that door is locked and bolted from the inside, it's impossible to break in," someone yelled.

But, as the men stared in shock, the door began to be torn off of its' hinges and right out of the wall.

In the empty doorway stood a giant creature.

"It's the Heap!" the chief scientist whispered in terror.

Growling, the creature strode over to the machine. With one massive motion it picked the machine up.

"Is it human?" asked the smallest scientist.

"If it ever was, it isn't anymore."

3

"My machine! It's going to destroy my machine!" The chief scientist started to run towards the monster. His colleagues grabbed him and held him back as the monster roared in anger.

Still roaring, the monster lifted the machine up over his head. Then it threw the machine against the lab wall. It exploded and the lab was awash with colored light as the delicate interiors of the scientist's invention crumbled away to nothing.

The four men stood staring at the remains of their work, in shock.

Then the monster stood up to its full height. It roared again, and this time the roar sounded almost like a laugh.

The monster turned away from the scientists and strode out of the lab doors and into the night.

4

The next night, four teenagers drove along the highway heading for campus. Biff, a handsome 16 year old was at the wheel. Next to him was his pretty friend, Kim. In the backseat sat Puggsy and his sidekick, Sherman Fangsworth, also known as "Fangs."

"Boy," Biff said, "I'm sure glad Sally and Professor Boyd invited us to the University science exhibit."

"I just hope we're not too late," said Kim, pointing to a story in the newspaper she was reading. "Have you seen this?"

"MONSTER STRIKES AGAIN!" read the newspaper's headline.

Biff looked worried, "That's the third time this week."

"Yes," said Kim, "and that leaves Sally Boyd's father the only Professor in the department who hasn't been attacked!"

5

Leaning forward, Fangs said, "Boy, that's enough to make you want to stay *away* from college."

"Your brains are enough to keep *you* away," sneered Puggsy.

"Oh yeah," said Fangs, "says who?"

Puggsy raised himself up in his seat and pressed his face against Fangs', nose to nose. "Says me," he said, pointing his thumb at his own chest.

Fangs backed down, "OK, OK, just checking."

Biff turned to the others, "Looks like we're going to fall into another adventure."

"Oh no," said Fangs, pulling his cap down over his ears.

"Don't worry, old pal," Puggsy said. "You have nothing to worry about with me around."

But Fangs just sank down in his seat, sulking.

6

The kids arrived at Professor Boyd's house and parked in the driveway out front.

Sally Boyd opened the front door. "Gosh, am I glad you guys are here. Did you read about the Heap?"

"We sure did," answered Biff, "and it looks like you could be next, Professor."

Boyd, a tall, grey-haired man, said, "Yes, I'm the only one who hasn't been attacked . . . yet."

"What about Professor Arnos, Dad?" asked Sally.

"But the college fired Professor Arnos long before the monster showed up, didn't they?" asked Kim.

"Well," said Professor Boyd, "Arnos was doing some unauthorized experiments."

Puggsy turned to the Professor, "Don't worry, if that Heap guy shows up here, we'll take care of him. We have a secret weapon!"

7

Fangs scratched his head. "We do?" he said, looking confused.

After dinner that night, the gang went to the living room. There they built a complicated contraption. They used nuts, bolts, pipes, a vacuum cleaner, lampshades, sheets, even the kitchen sink. The machine took up almost the entire living room.

"This should do it," said Puggsy, putting his hammer down. "If old ugly face shows up, this trap will take care of him!"

Biff, who had been standing with Fangs, watching Puggsy work on the machine said, "Right, and we'll be hiding and ready to jump him."

Fangs got so excited at the thought of an adventure that he started jumping around, boxing with his shadow. "Yeah, I'll give him a right, then a left, then I'll…"

8

"Freeze it!" roared Puggsy.

"O.K. Puggs, don't get mad." whispered Fangs.

"Time to activate our secret weapon, Puggsy." said Biff, taking out a postcard of a moonlit night.

Puggsy showed Fangs the postcard. "Here, Fangs, take a look at the moon." he said.

Suddenly, Fangs' eyes widened to a blank stare. Then his pupils started whirling crazily. Fangs' arms began to move and soon he was spinning like a top . . . and roaring!

When Fangs stopped spinning he had become the "secret weapon." For whenever Sherman Fangsworth sees a picture of the moon he becomes *Fangface,* a weird and wacky werewolf!

9

While the kids were still downstairs with the recently transformed Fangs, a more sinister monster was making his way through an open bedroom window.

Creeping quietly along the corridor, the Heap found his way to the Professor's study where Boyd was going over notes for one of his classes.

Before Professor Boyd knew what had happened, the Heap had grabbed him and tossed him over his shoulder like a sack of coal.

"Help, help!" cried the Professor as the Heap hurriedly carried him to an open window.

Downstairs, Biff was the first to react to the cry. "It's the Professor, and I'll bet the Heap has him! Come on Fangface, let's get that turkey!"

10

Fangface's mouth opened wide and he got a hungry look on his face.

"Umm, turkey," he snarled, "I love turkey!"

And before anyone could stop him, Fangface had zipped out of sight. Biff and Kim ran after him and finally found him sitting on the floor. His mouth was stretched out and it looked like Puggsy was inside!

"Oh no," said Kim, "whenever Fangface sees or hears of food, he swallows Puggsy."

Biff said, "Fangface, let Puggs out. The Heap is getting away!"

"Help, get me out of here," yelled Puggsy.

But Fangface stubbornly shook his head no.

11

"Well," said Biff, "there's only one way." He pushed Fangface down and sat down on top of him.

Fangface pounded on the floor like a wrestler while Biff rubbed the soles of his feet.

"This will calm him down," he said.

It worked, Fangface got a peaceful look in his eyes and began to relax.

"O.K. Fangface, let him out," said Biff.

Fangface opened his mouth and Puggsy came charging out. "Lemme at im, lemme at 'im! When I get through with him, he's gonna be a fur coat!" Puggsy yelled.

"Forget it, Puggs." Biff said. "Come on, we have to get the Heap!"

12

With Fangface at the lead, the kids ran up the stairs.

The Heap reached the window just as Fangface got to the top of the stairs. Snarling and yapping, Fangface put on full speed to catch the Heap. The Heap climbed through the window but Fangface was catching up fast.

Now the Heap was out the window and carrying the Professor with him as he climbed down a big tree just outside the house. Never slowing down, Fangface flew right through the window after the Heap. Then it happened! Whump! Fangface flew right back into the house, backwards!

He had hit a giant branch of the tree outside which catapulted him back through the window. Still going backwards, Fangface hit the bannister and slid fast, heading for the living room.

13

"Watch out, Fangface," shouted Biff. "You're heading for our trap!"

But it was too late. Fangface flew right into the trap, landing with a loud crash.

The contraption started working, pulling Fangface through the pipes, making them bulge.

Finally, Fangface popped up out of the kitchen sink with a lampshade on his head and water spouting out of his ears.

The kids rushed up to him.

"Are you O.K.?" asked Puggsy. "Say something, old pal."

Fangface snarled, "Turn off the water . . . please."

Puggsy turned the spout off and water stopped coming from Fangface's ears.

14

"The Heap got away." said Biff as he dried Fangface off.

"Snarl . . . yeah," sighed a lightly bruised Fangface.

Sally Boyd looked sad, "I'll probably never see my father again."

"Sure you will, Sally." Biff put his hand on Sally's shoulder. "We'll find your father, and the Heap too!"

"Yeah," said Puggsy, "No monster's going to make monkeys out of us."

"Monkeys, snarl, we're no monkeys," said Fangface—all the while doing his monkey imitation.

"Come on," said Biff, "if we leave now we can follow the Heap's footprints. Everybody into the Wolfcar."

15

Far down the road, at the base of a mountain, the Heap was nearing his secret hide-out. His huge, hairy feet made deep prints in the mud around the mountain.

Holding Professor Boyd over his shoulder, the Heap walked up to a huge rock. It was covering the entrance to the mountain.

Standing in front of the rock, the Heap moved a loose stone away from the mountain wall. Behind the stone was a switch. He pressed the switch and the large rock covering the cave entrance rolled up, like a garage door.

The Heap entered the dark, mountain cave. When he was inside, the rock-door closed silently behind him.

The Heap carried Professor Boyd down the silent mountain corridor.

16

At the end of the corridor, the Heap stopped to open a door. Beyond the door was a laboratory. Professor Boyd's eyes widened in amazement as he saw the well equipped lab. It was brightly lit and in the middle of the floor sat a Ray Machine with many knobs and dials.

The Heap carried Professor Boyd over to a cell which was built into one wall of the lab. He put Professor Boyd down in the cell and locked the door, hanging the key out of the Professor's reach.

Laughing evilly, the Heap strode to the center of the room and turned on the Ray Machine. The machine rattled and began to cast a strange green glow over the entire room.

17

As the green light from the machine became even brighter, the Heap began to fade away. Suddenly, in a flash of light, the Heap was gone and in his place stood Professor Arnos, a small man wearing horn rimmed glasses.

"I don't believe it," whispered Professor Boyd, who had been watching in awe.

"You can believe it, Boyd," sneered the mad Professor Arnos. "It's true. You and the others thought I was a fool but now you see what I have invented. You laughed at me but I will get my revenge. I have perfected a Ray Machine that can turn humans into any form I want. I am going to change you all, the entire faculty, into hulking monsters!"

18

Meanwhile, the Wolfcar moved slowly down the road. Biff was driving while Kim looked for footprints out the window. In the back seat, Fangface sat happily on Puggsy's shoulders.

"It seems like we've been driving forever," said Kim. "Where do these footprints end?"

"Right up ahead!" Biff pointed in front of him. "The road and the tracks end right up against that mountain."

Biff parked the car and everyone piled out.

"There must be some sort of secret entrance nearby," Kim said.

"Come on, Fangs, let's see if we can find it." said Puggsy.

"Sure thing, snarl, Puggs. We'll find it." Fangface started looking for an entrance.

19

"You guys check out the mountainside. Kim and I will look around the rocks and shrubs." said Biff.

Puggs and Fangface went off, feeling along the mountain wall for loose rocks. Fangface knocked on the big rock that blocked the cave entrance, listening for a hollow sound.

"Maybe this thing goes up like a garage door." said Puggsy. While Puggsy stood looking at the rock, the loose stone fell away, revealing the hidden switch. Fangface pulled the switch.

The rock went up—and so did Puggsy when his belt got caught on the rough edge of the boulder. "What the . . . get me down from here!" he shouted.

Fangface found a big stone and threw it up to Puggsy. Puggsy caught the stone and its weight pulled him down. He landed with a loud thump.

"I got ya down Puggs. I did good, right?" said Fangface.

20

"Yeah, next time do me a favor, though. Leave me up there." said Puggsy rolling his eyes.

Puggsy slowly got to his feet as Kim and Biff ran up to the cave entrance.

"Nice going," said Biff, "you found the hidden entrance. Now let's see what's inside."

The four walked inside the cave. It was very dark and very scary. Odd rocks hung from the cave roof and the cavern branched into several different tunnels leading deep inside the mountain.

Biff was the first to speak, "If we're ever going to find Professor Boyd, we'll have to split up."

Fangface put his arm around Puggsy and rested his head on his shoulder. "Snarl—me and Puggsy —growl. Partners!"

"If I had my choice," Puggsy muttered, "I think I'd rather be partners with the Heap."

21

Biff and Kim took the path to their right while Puggsy and Fangface began walking down the path to their left.

The path Biff and Kim took was dark and foreboding. Cobwebs hung from above them and small animals scurried across the floor. Every now and then a small stone would fall from overhead.

They walked for a very long time, searching for some sign of the Heap and Professor Boyd.

Suddenly they saw it! Far down the corridor a light was shining.

"Come on, Kim," Biff said, "maybe that light is a clue."

They both hurried down the corridor, toward the light.

22

As they got nearer to the light they saw that it was coming from underneath a large door.

The door was very heavy. Biff pushed hard with his shoulder and little by little the door opened.

Finally Biff and Kim stood in the open doorway.

"Jeepers," said Kim, "a whole underground lab!"

Biff pointed to the cell in the far wall of the lab, "And look, there's Professor Boyd!"

They walked into the lab, which seemed empty except for the Professor. By the cell door they found a key.

"Don't worry, Professor, we'll get you out." Kim said as she opened the cell door.

Suddenly a shadow loomed up from behind them.

"May I help you?" said Professor Arnos.

Startled, Biff and Kim spun around. Before they could resist, Professor Arnos had pushed them into the cell and locked the door.

"What's the big idea?" shouted Biff. "Who are you, anyway?"

"I'm afraid that's your monster." said Professor Boyd.

"He's right," said Arnos. "And when I get through, the University will be sorry it ever fired me."

"Oh yeah," said Kim. "When Fangface catches up with you . . ."

Biff quickly put his hand over her mouth, but it was too late.

Arnos moved in front of the Ray Machine, "So there *are* others!" he said.

24

The frail Professor Arnos stood in front of his Ray Machine. He flicked a switch on the machine's side and the strange green light began to glow. In front of the stunned eyes of Kim and Biff, Professor Arnos once again turned into the terrifying creature, the Heap!

"I wish we could warn Puggsy and Fangface," whispered Kim.

"There's no way," said Biff. "The Heap's got us *all* in a heap of trouble!"

Professor Arnos, now turned into the Heap, stepped away from the Ray Machine. Growling, he lumbered slowly to the lab doors. As he walked out of the laboratory and into the cave tunnel his blood-chilling growl became an even more chilling laugh.

25

Meanwhile, in another part of the cave, Fangface and Puggsy crept down a dark and spooky corridor.

Fangface was very frightened, "We'll never find our way around these caves, Puggs. Never, never, never!"

"Aw shaddup!" snapped Puggsy, who was more frightened then he would have liked to admit.

"What should I do, Puggs, what should I do?" asked Fangface.

"Just keep your peepers open and follow me." Puggsy said. "My keen sense of direction tells me that this is the safest way."

26

Puggsy and Fangface kept walking silently down the long corridor.

Suddenly a giant figure loomed up ahead of them. Roaring with anger, the beast stood up to his full height, beating on his chest like an ape.

"It's the Heap!" yelled Puggsy. "Go get him, Fangface."

And that's just what Fangface did. He ran right at the hulking monster and picked him up, lifting him high in the air.

"I got him, Puggs, I got him." snarled Fangface. "Now what do I do?"

"Are you nuts?" yelled Puggsy. "Drop him, we better get out of here!"

Fangface dropped the Heap and began running after Puggsy.

The Heap picked himself up off the floor and lumbered down the corridor, chasing them both.

27

"Hurry up, Fangface," Puggsy yelled, "he's gaining on us."

Puggsy and Fangface kept running. They changed directions, darting and weaving through the halls but the Heap was still close behind.

"Hey Puggs," panted Fangface, "where are we going?"

"I don't know," answered Puggsy. "Hey, look up there. It looks like a ladder leading to a trap door. Follow me, Fangface, this may be our way out."

Puggsy and Fangface scooted up the ladder till they reached the trap door in the roof.

At the top of the ladder Puggsy reached up. He pushed open the door and looked up. All he saw was darkness. He felt like he was under a lid or something.

28

It *was* a lid that he was under. Someone lifted the lid off of his head and Puggsy saw that he was in the middle of a restaurant. As a matter of fact, he was in the middle of somebody's dinner, in the middle of a table, in the middle of a restaurant. And he had a roast duck on his head!

"Sorry, miss," Puggsy said, jumping out of the trap door and carrying the table with him like a skirt.

Feeling the duck on his head he reached for it, "Here's your duck, lady." he said.

"Duck! Duck is food!" shouted Fangface as he poked his head out of the trap door.

Thinking fast, Puggsy tied a napkin around Fangface's eyes and led him into the kitchen.

The Heap jumped out of the trap door and followed Puggsy and Fangface into the kitchen. All he saw there was a big, hairy person washing dishes in a sink full of suds. What the Heap didn't know was that the big, hairy person was none other then our friend, Fangface.

The Heap snuck up behind Fangface, who was so surprised that he spun around and threw a whole armful of suds right on the Heap.

Angry and sopping wet, the Heap ran out of the kitchen's back door.

As soon as the Heap was gone, Fangface reached into the sink and pulled out Puggsy, who had been hiding in the suds and was now even wetter than the Heap.

30

"I hid you good, didn't I, Puggsy?" said Fangface.

"Yeah," said Puggsy, "but did you have to use me as a dishcloth? Never mind, just get me dried off."

Fangface picked Puggsy up and wrang him out, like a towel, "OK Puggs, whatever you say."

"Next time, remind me to bring a blow dryer." said Puggs, still unwinding. Then he pointed to the back door. "Now get after that Heap, and this time use a net!"

Fangface grabbed a large net that was hanging on the kitchen wall and charged for the back door. "Don't worry, I'll get him this time," he snarled.

31

Fangface ran out the door with Puggsy close behind him.

There was the Heap, standing with his back turned and searching through the trash cans for his prey.

The Heap roared and snarled as he threw around the cans. He made so much noise that he didn't hear Fangface and Puggsy come through the back door.

Fangface snuck up behind the Heap, raising the net over his head. Finally, when he was right behind the monster he took a quick look around him to make sure the coast was clear.

Then it happened. Someone had taped a picture postcard to one of the backyard walls. It was a picture of the sun.

32

Whenever Sherman Fangsworth sees a picture of the moon he becomes Fangface *but* whenever Fangface sees a picture of the sun he turns right back into meek and mild Sherman Fangsworth.

So, when Fangface saw the sunny postcard his eyes began whirling, then he began spinning like a top and Fangface was gone. In his place stood Sherman Fangsworth.

Staring at the Heap he said, "Hey what am I doing out here with big, blue and ugly?"

When Puggsy saw what had happened, he grabbed Fangs by the hand and threw him into a nearby empty trash can. Then Puggsy climbed in and the can began rolling out onto the street.

"As long as we have this thing going we may as well head back for the cave," said Puggsy.

33

Biff, Kim and Professor Boyd jumped up in their cell when they heard the Heap return.

"Puggsy and Fangface must have gotten away," whispered Biff.

"Yes, but the Heap sure looks like a sore loser," said Kim.

The Heap lumbered over to them. He pushed a button on the side of the wall outside the cell.

As Biff, Kim and Professor Boyd screamed in fright, the cell walls began to slowly close in on them."

"Boy, he really *is* a sore loser!" said Kim. "When these walls slam shut we're going to be thinner than a stack of pancakes. Maybe he'll change his mind."

Biff shook his head, "Not a chance, the only ones who can save us now are Puggsy and Fangface, wherever they are."

34

At that moment the trash can containing Puggsy and Fangs rolled to a stop against a small boulder near the Heap's cave.

"Nice going," Puggs said, "it only took you an hour to get us here."

"Can I help it if I took a wrong turn?" said Fangs. "I've never driven a trash can before."

"Alright, alright, forget it," said Puggsy. "Where do you think Biff and Kim are? They were supposed to meet us here."

"I don't see them Puggs. Do you think the Heap got them?" asked Fangs.

"I don't know, but we better find out." answered Puggsy. "Let's check out the cave."

With Fangs in the lead, they crept down the long cave hall. Finally they came to the lab.

35

Puggsy and Fangface walked into the lab. There they saw Biff, Kim and Professor Boyd, with the cell walls still closing in on them.

"Puggsy, Fangs, help us. We're about to be crushed!" yelled Biff.

"What we need now," Puggsy said, "is the cunning and prowess of an animal!" He pulled out a picture of the moon and showed it to Fangs.

Whirling and spinning, Fangs turned into Fangface.

"Quick, Fangface," Kim called, "get us out of here!"

Fangface grabbed the cell doors and with one mighty pull, tore it off of its' hinges.

They rushed out of the cell, just as the walls closed.

"Whew," sighed Biff, "that was a close call!"

"What happened, you guys?" asked Fangface.

36

Before anyone could answer, the Heap burst into the room. Roaring with rage he picked up the Ray Machine and began running.

"He's getting away," yelled Professor Boyd.

The kids took off after him.

"We've got you cornered, Professor Arnos," said Biff. "Now give us the Ray Machine."

The Heap roared back angrily and pressed a different button on the side of the machine. The cave wall opened, revealing a hidden door. The Heap ran out the door.

Puggsy and Fangface dashed to catch the Heap but it was too late, the cave wall closed before they could reach it.

"He got away," Kim said. "And what is he going to do next?"

37

"What do we do now?" sighed Kim. "The Heap is still on the loose—and he has that terrible machine with him."

"Well let's get out of this creepy cave, first," said Biff. "Everyone into the Wolfcar, we're going back to Professor Boyd's."

Arriving at the Professor's house, the gang gathered in the living room to discuss strategy.

"If that Heap plans on turning the entire faculty into monsters, he'll have to put the Ray Machine in a high place," said Biff.

The Professor snapped his fingers, "The University radio tower is the perfect place. It's the tallest building on campus!"

"That must be it," said Biff. "Call the sheriff and tell him to meet us at the radio tower. We've got to get that Heap—before he gets us!"

38

Biff drove everyone to the campus in the Wolfcar. Fangface sat on Puggsy's shoulders in the back seat. Kim looked up as soon as they reached the radio tower. "There he is. There's the Heap and he has the Ray Machine!"

Fangface growled, "Puggsy and I'll take care of him."

"We've got to get the Ray Machine before he uses it on everyone on campus," said Kim. "Puggs and Fangface take the elevator to the roof. Biff and I will block his escape from down here."

Puggsy raced into the Science Building with Fangface still on his shoulders. He took the elevator to the roof.

When they reached the roof, Puggsy looked up at Fangface, "You can get off now," he said.

"No!" Fangface snarled stubbornly.

39

"This calls for the old mirror trick," Puggsy thought to himself as he pulled out a mirror. Whenever Fangface sees his own image he goes bananas.

Puggsy showed Fangface the mirror.

Fangface started howling like a dog and chasing his tail. Then he took a running start and leaped onto the radio tower, after the Heap.

The Heap saw Fangface coming and, still holding the Ray Machine, jumped from the tower back onto the Science Building roof.

Flapping his arms wildly, Fangface sailed right after him.

Now all three were on the Science Building roof, Fangface, the Heap and Puggsy, who was waiting by the elevator.

Kim and Biff watched anxiously from below.

40

Fangface caught up with the monster on the building roof. "I'll take that," he said, grabbing the Ray Machine out of the Heap's hands.

"Hurry, Fangface, to the elevator," yelled Puggsy.

Fangface ran for the elevator, reaching it just in time. The elevator doors slammed shut.

The Heap reached the elevator just after the doors closed. He ripped the doors open, but Fangface and Puggsy were already going down in the elevator car.

The Heap roared once and then jumped into the elevator shaft, grabbing hold of the cables. He began sliding down the elevator cables, heading for Puggsy and Fangface. Looking up out of the trap door in the elevator car roof, Puggsy saw the Heap.

"Fangface," Puggsy yelled, "the Heap's still after us!"

41

As soon as the elevator reached the ground floor, Fangface started running. He was in such a hurry that he didn't wait for the doors to open. He just stuck his feet through the elevator floor and ran, wearing the elevator like a coat.

The Heap was close behind.

Fangface and Puggsy—and the elevator—ran for a nearby air field. Fangface tripped and the elevator flew into the air, landing on an air-rocket and activating its engine. The rocket took off with the elevator.

The Heap, seeing what had happened, jumped onto the top of the elevator just as it took off.

"Follow that elevator," yelled Kim as Biff started up the Wolfcar.

42

Inside the elevator, Puggsy and Fangface didn't know they were flying.

"I think we ditched him," said Puggsy. "Give me that machine and let's get out of here."

Puggsy stepped casually out of the elevator, but there was nothing to step out on!

"Yipes, we're airborne," Puggsy cried, looking down. He dropped the Ray Machine and, churning his legs wildly, made it back into the elevator.

Down below, Biff drove the Wolf-car back and forth, trying to get under the falling Ray Machine. He handed Kim an old baseball mitt from the glove compartment.

"Good catch," he said, as Kim grabbed the Ray Machine.

43

The air rocket, flying wildly, finally crashed into the radio tower, depositing the elevator on top.

Opening the trap door, the Heap entered the elevator. He grabbed Puggsy, but just as he did the elevator began to teeter. The Heap started sliding out of the elevator, still holding Puggsy's arms.

Fangface grabbed Puggsy's feet as the Heap started pulling Puggs out of the elevator.

Now all three were hanging from the elevator. Fangface had his feet hooked behind the elevator doors. He held on to Puggsy's big toe. The Heap had Puggsy by the arms.

On the ground, Kim and Biff quickly set up the Ray Machine. They aimed the ray right at the Heap and pushed the button marked, 'activate'.

44

When the green ray hit the Heap he began changing into Professor Arnos.

"Help, get me down from here," shouted the transformed Arnos. "I'm going to fall."

Using all his strength, Fangface pulled slowly. Finally he got Puggsy and Professor Arnos back into the elevator car.

"Now that the Heap is changed into Professor Arnos, he's a lot lighter," Biff said to Kim.

"Nice going, Fangface," Puggsy said. "That was close!"

"You said it, pal," Fangface snarled back.

Puggsy, Fangface, and Arnos took the stairs down to meet Biff and Kim.

45

Waiting on the ground were Biff, Kim, Sally, Professor Boyd, and the police.

As a policeman led Arnos into a paddy wagon Professor Boyd turned to the gang, "I don't know how to thank you kids." he said.

"Yes," said Sally, "if it wasn't for you, that Heap would have caused a disaster."

"Well, you helped too," Kim said.

"That's right," said Biff, "you can't *let us* take all the credit."

Suddenly they heard a gulp.

"Oops," Kim said, "Fangface thought you said *lettuce* and I think he just made himself a Puggsy sandwich! We better show him a picture of the sun."

46

"Here, Fangface, take a look at the sun," said Biff, showing Fangface a postcard.

As soon as he saw the picture, Fangface began spinning like a top, soon he was just plain Sherman Fangsworth again.

"Huh? What's happening? What are you made up to look like a sandwich for, Puggs? It's not Halloween." Fangs said.

"When I get my hands on you," Puggsy sputtered, "you'll think it's the Fourth of July."

Still dressed as a sandwich, Puggsy took up after Fangs.

As the two ran down the road, Biff turned to Kim, "Looks like everything's back to normal." he said. And the whole Fangface gang started to laugh.